Little Stupendo longs for the day when she too can perform magnificent stunts like her dad, the Great Stupendo, the world's Number One stuntman. And that day comes sooner than she expects!

Jon Blake started writing for children during his brief career as a teacher. Since then he has had a number of jobs, from community centre warden to part-time lecturer. He is the author of several books for young people, including *Geoffrey's First*, *Holiday in Happy Street*, *The King of Rock and Roll* and *The Hell Hound of Hooley Street*, as well as the picture books *Impo* and *You're a Hero, Daley B!* He has also written plays for television and the stage.

Martin Chatterton's illustrations have appeared in lots of magazines and books. He teaches graphics and illustration at a number of colleges.

Books by the same author

You're a Hero, Daley B!
Impo

For older readers

The Hell Hound of Hooley Street
How I Became a Star
The King of Rock and Roll
The Likely Stories

JON BLAKE

Illustrations by Martin Chatterton

WALKER BOOKS
AND SUBSIDIARIES
LONDON • BOSTON • SYDNEY

First published 1995 by
Walker Books Ltd, 87 Vauxhall Walk
London SE11 5HJ

This edition published 1995

2 4 6 8 10 9 7 5 3

Text © 1995 Jon Blake
Illustrations © 1995 Martin Chatterton

This book has been typeset in Garamond.

Printed in England

British Library Cataloguing in Publication Data
A catalogue record for this book
is available from the British Library.

ISBN 0-7445-4300-2

CONTENTS

PART 1

In a huge stadium, somewhere on Earth, the Great Stupendo was about to perform his latest stunt.

A hush fell over the crowd. The Great Stupendo revved up his bike.

9

He sped down the track like a bullet.

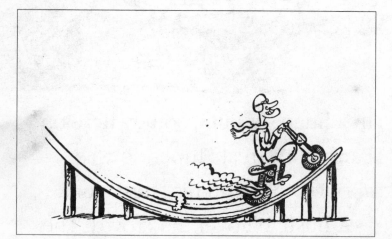

He raced up the ramp like wildfire.

10

He flew into the air like a jet plane.

High over the cars he sailed.

Then SMASH!

He crashed to the ground,
bounced off his bike, and ripped his
trousers.

Everyone
cheered wildly.
Everyone, that is,
except the Great
Stupendo's
daughter, Little
Stupendo.

That's another costume I'll have to mend.

After the show, the Stupendos
went home. As usual, the Great
Stupendo took a nap. He took his
motorbike with him, because he
always slept with his motorbike.

Little Stupendo sulked. She wished she could sleep with a motorbike. In fact, she secretly wished she could do stunts as well. It was much more interesting than mending trousers.

Little Stupendo
went into the yard.
She climbed the
shed and pretended
it was a skyscraper.

She trained the
cat and pretended
it was a tiger.

Then she peeped
over at next door's
washing line.

I could pretend
that was a
high wire.

Mr Chinspot lived next door. He was a tall, thin, suspicious old man. He preferred to be left in peace with his matchstick models.

"What is it now?" he grumbled.

Suddenly there
was a loud scream.
It came from the
Stupendos' house.

Little Stupendo
went hurrying
back inside with
Mr Chinspot
following. They
found the Great
Stupendo in
the bathroom,
shaking all over.

A th-thing!
A th-thing, in
the plughole!

Little Stupendo hardly dared look. Was it a snake? A scorpion? A sewer rat?

Actually, it was none of these things. It was a tiny, harmless, frightened spider. Little Stupendo put a tooth-mug over it and slid a postcard under it. Then she threw it out of the window.

The Great Stupendo calmed down. He turned to Mr Chinspot with a solemn warning: "No one else must ever know about my secret fear," he said.

PART 2

A week passed. Then it was time for
the Great Stupendo's next stunt.
For this he needed a barrel, so he
went off to Barrels-R-Us to buy one.
Little Stupendo went too. She had
shopping of her own to do.

Near the shops, they saw a poster
which made the Great Stupendo's
teeth gnash together:

The Great Stupendo looked both ways, then drew glasses on Johnny Bravo, and scribbled RUBBISH all over the poster.

Johnny Bravo, as you may have guessed, was the Great Stupendo's greatest rival.

Still sulking, the Great Stupendo went into Barrels-R-Us. "I want a barrel," he grunted. "Please," he added.

The saleswoman nodded. "Is that a barrel for beer?" she asked. "Or for rainwater?"

"It is a barrel," replied the Great Stupendo, "for myself."

The Great Stupendo measured himself against the barrels till he found one big enough to curl up in.

Back home, the Great Stupendo began to climb into the barrel. Then he had a nasty thought:

The Great Stupendo shuddered. He called for Little Stupendo, but Little Stupendo was still out shopping. There was only one person he could ask for help – Mr Chinspot.

As usual, Mr Chinspot was working on a matchstick model. He wasn't at all happy to be disturbed.

"Could you please climb into this barrel?" asked the Great Stupendo.

Mr Chinspot was suspicious. "What for?" he grunted.

"To check there are no ... *things* in it," replied the Great Stupendo.

I hope this isn't some kind of trick.

The Great Stupendo fetched a chair. Mr Chinspot got onto it and, with some difficulty, climbed into the barrel.

The Great Stupendo went off to change. Mr Chinspot peered about in the dim light. It was hard even to see his own feet.

Meanwhile, a van arrived outside.
Two workmen got out and went
into the Great Stupendo's house.

They fitted the lid on the barrel
and carried it off to their van.

Mr Chinspot didn't know what was going on. He banged and he shouted, but no one seemed to hear.

Suddenly he felt himself moving, very fast.

Then he heard the sound of an excited crowd.

Next he seemed to be floating, quite calmly and gently.

"Actually," he thought to himself, "this is quite pleasant."

Next second...

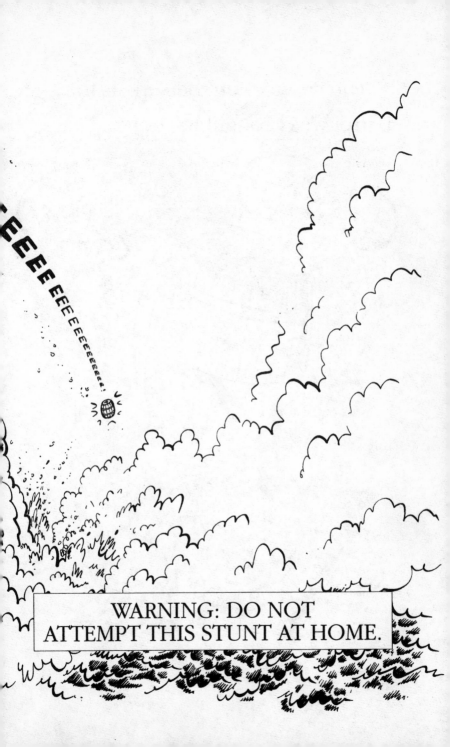

The crowd went berserk as the
barrel was brought to shore.

Suddenly, however, the cheers stopped, and there was a stunned silence. The man in the barrel was not the Great Stupendo!

Mr Chinspot dusted himself down, shook himself out, and frowned a deadly frown.

The Great Stupendo did this on purpose!

And with that, Mr Chinspot vowed to get his revenge.

PART 3

Next day, the Great Stupendo
went to see Vanessa Gabble, his
agent. Vanessa was the person who
organized the stunts.

Vanessa looked worried. She
showed a newspaper to the Great
Stupendo.

The next newspaper was

even worse.

"There is only one thing for it," said Vanessa. "We must make sure your next stunt is so fantastic that Johnny Bravo can never follow it."

"But what shall I do?" asked the Great Stupendo.

Vanessa showed the Great
Stupendo a photo. It was a picture
of a mighty canyon – Vulture
Canyon, a hundred metres wide
and four kilometres deep.

The Great Stupendo gasped.

That was a truly scary thought,
even for the Great Stupendo.

Back at home, the Great
Stupendo began to practise.

First he put a
plank between
two chairs
and walked
across that.

Then he put a
broomstick
between two
step-ladders.

"Now I need something more
difficult," he said to himself.

36

Out in the yard, Little Stupendo was putting up a new clothes line.

Little Stupendo wasn't very pleased when the Great Stupendo got up on her new line. He even used her clothes-line pole for balance. He practised all day, till the sun went down, then went off to bed with his motorbike.

"I'll show him," said Little Stupendo to herself.

As the Great Stupendo snored in his bed, Little Stupendo walked the plank. Then the broomstick. By the light of the moon, she crept outside and climbed onto the clothes line. Bit by bit, she learned how to keep her balance. She even waved to the crowd, except no one was watching.

No one, that is, except

Little Stupendo almost fell off the
line. Then she saw it was only her
old neighbour.

Mr Chinspot's brain began to tick
over. A plan formed in his mind.
It was the plan for his revenge.

Next day, Mr Chinspot paid a visit
to 333 Sunset Villas.

333 Sunset Villas was the home of
Johnny Bravo.

Mr Chinspot rang the bell.

As usual, Johnny Bravo was
riding his bike round the house.
The bike had two huge mirrors, so
Johnny could watch himself
everywhere he went.

Johnny bumped down the stairs, did a wheelie through the hall and almost made Mr Chinspot jump out of his socks.

Mr Chinspot leaned closer and whispered in Johnny Bravo's ear. A big, broad smile spread across Johnny's face.

PART 4

At last it was the morning of the
great event. All was dim and still
and silent at Vulture Canyon. Then,
as if from nowhere, a helicopter
appeared.

MORE WALKER SPRINTERS
For You to Enjoy

☐ 0-7445-3664-2 *Gemma and the Beetle People*
by Enid Richemont/
Tony Kenyon   £2.99

☐ 0-7445-3188-8 *Beware Olga!*
by Gillian Cross/
Arthur Robins   £3.50

☐ 0-7445-3196-9 *Captain Cranko and the Crybaby*
by Jean Ure/
Mick Brownfield   £3.50

☐ 0-7445-3095-4 *Millie Morgan, Pirate*
by Margaret Ryan/
Caroline Church   £3.50

☐ 0-7445-3173-X *Jolly Roger*
by Colin McNaughton   £3.50